D1491595

21st-Century Playground Edition

Pimp
Your
Vocab

21st-Century Playground Edition

Pimp
Your
Vocab

**A Terrifying Dictionary of the Words
Kids Don't Want You to Know**

LUCY TOBIN

PORTICO

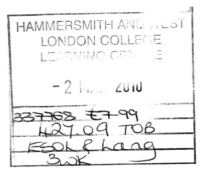

To Mum, Dad, Anna, Rob, Justin, Resa, Ella & Lily and Howard.

First published in the United Kingdom in 2009 by
Portico Books
10 Southcombe Street
London
W14 0RA

An imprint of Anova Books Company Ltd

ISBN 9781906032722

A CIP catalogue record for this book is available from the British Library.

10 9 8 7 6 5 4 3 2 1

Typeset by SX Composing DTP, Rayleigh, Essex
Printed and bound by Times Offset, Malaysia

This book can be ordered direct from the publisher at www.anovabooks.com

Contents

Yer but no but whatever.

Vicky Pollard, *Little Britain*.

Introduction

Visiting a school earlier this year, I overheard a teacher asking his student how his English GCSE exams had gone. 'Bit worried, actually,' was the boy's response. 'Think the whole thing will make me look like a massive fudge.'

A piece of fudge would have done better in the exam perhaps, since the boy clearly couldn't differentiate between language to address a friend and a teacher, but that wasn't what he had meant.

'A fudge?' the bemused teacher replied – 'did you come out of the exam sticky and brown?' 'Er, no sir – a fudge, like, you know – an idiot – the letters in the word fudge will probably be my grade . . . *geddit*?'

Geddit indeed – what with grade inflation these days the boy probably got an A* – and opened his results letter with the exclamation 'immense!'

Confused? You're probably over thirty.

Word on the (teen) street now is that while some things are still 'cool' more are increasingly likely to be 'the beast'.

Someone who is 'sick' is 'cool', not ill. Duh.

If someone is flatroofing then they're working

hard, not training as a roofer. Obv. And 'kaka' is totally *not* the sweet sound of a baby gurgling, but a teenager saying something is shit. That's shit like really bad, not literally poo.

Keep up at the back!

While teenspeak is pockmarked by the word 'standard' (see page 94), it is very different from Standard English. It's so diverse that an updated version of Orwell's *1984* would require talk police and translators as well as thought police.

Language changes fast – and that can scare the hell out of parents, teachers and anyone who no longer braves the clubs on a Friday night for fear of being 'too old'.

But teens are not alone in adapting language to forge a sense of individuality – there's a long historical precedent. The English language is continually changing: the most recent update of the *Oxford English Dictionary* involved 2,693 revisions and additions of words.

Teenglish words (as they are known, though not by their users) are often the result of inspired neologisms. Who can fail to smile at the concept of an 'ohnosecond', that sudden instant of time when you realise you have done something stupid? Or the idea of a McPee – going to use the toilet somewhere you're not allowed really. And Teenglish's verbicide –

when words are weakened through indiscriminate use – means that 'rape' is now used in relation to vandalising someone's internet status (see 'Facebook rape' p. 38).

With Standard English we can often read rapidly without focusing 'in waht oredr the ltteers in a wrod are' because what is important is 'the frist and lsat ltteer be at the rghit pclae'. In communicating with a Teenglish-speaking randomer (that's an outsider to your social group) their words can seem like a new language. Meaning is not an exact science, but depends on mutual agreement between reader and writer, speaker and listener, teenager and adult. So, to bridge the communication gap between teachers and students, parents and kids, here is a compilation, a terrifying celebration if you will, of *the* cool words of the moment to help you pimp your vocab.

Pimping Your Vocab:
A User's Guide

Back in the day (that's the '90s, duh – *so* last century), bad meant good and wicked meant cool and kids would go round each other's gaff and chillax. But that's already old school. Today's playgrounds are splattered with new words – now dark means bad, mint means good, down is hip, the old gaff is the new crib and cotching is the new chillaxing.

In order to speak to teenagers (and kidults) these days you need to be well versed in language, and not just the OED variety. It's a good start if you know how to speak English, but even then you still have a *long* way to go. And don't think that you'll be 'down' with the 'crew' just by reading this book – you won't – you still have to work on it. Before trying these words out on the street, you have to appear 'street'.

So make like a teenager: slam the door to your bedroom and refuse to let anyone in. Chuck your clothes out of the wardrobe into heaps on the floor, then, take out this book, familiarise yourself with the words phonetically – how you deliver them is just as important as what they mean, *obv* – and practise, practise, practise.

Remember, though, this is the language of kids, the yoof, the teens of today – so add a snarl, sneak in a spot of sarcasm, pretend you just don't care, and remember, learning is meant to be fun.

A and B the C of D *(ay-an'd-bee-the-cee-ov-dee)* – stands for above and beyond the call of duty.

　　As used in the sentence: *'You want me to tidy my room? No way man . . . that's A and B the C of D.'*

Addy *(add-dee)* – address. Refers mainly to your email address, but can still be used for postal address in emergencies.

　　As used in the sentence: *(1) 'I'm coming round . . . What's your addy?'*

　　(2) 'Give us your addy. I need your deets, like, now.'

Aggro *(agg-roe)* – hassle. Contraction of aggravation.

As used in the sentence: *'Jim went mental, so we were massively late – the whole day was aggro.'*

Ai *(ay)* – yes. To come to an agreement; from the Scottish 'aye' – possibly. Made famous, of course, by Ali G and now so popular that most adults will admit to using it freely.

As used in the conversation: *'Did you see dem kids at school?' 'Ai'.*

Air / Airing *(ay-r)* – talking rubbish or showing off. Can also be used when a person does not respond to another's comment.

As used in the sentence: *'WTF you on about? Are you airing me? I reckon you just chatting air, man.'*

Allie *(ah-lee)* – a response that indicates agreement, similar to 'innit', or the standard teenage grunt.

As used in the conversation: *'Doncha think his mum is well ming?' 'Allie.'*

Alligator *(ah-lee-gay-tor)* – someone, usually a female teenager, who spreads rumours or allegations about someone else. A gossip queen.

As used in the sentence: *'This stuff came out of nowhere – who did the talking? We need to track down the alligator. I'm gonna go apeshit.'*

Allow (that) *(ah-lao-that)* – a negative response; 'no way'.

Author's note: You might want to watch out for this one, because it's pretty much the opposite of what it seems. You might allow your most-loved teenage son/daughter to have a sleepover – but if their response is 'allow that', then they think their crib just isn't cool enough to show off to the crew.

As used in the conversation: *'Wanna go halves on this chocolate?' 'Allow that, man, not happening.'*

Apeshit *(ayp-shit)* – to show anger and annoyance at something/someone. Very rarely means the waste product of an ape (or other monkey-based lifeform).

As used in the sentence: *'Kate's rents found out about the dope – they've gone apeshit.'*

Arm candy (*ahm-can-dee*) – a hot male or female who accompanies someone for a particular event or party, but is not dating them exclusively. Can be used more generally to describe someone who is fit, but doesn't have much going on upstairs – or, in other words, is a bimbo/himbo.

As used in the sentence: '*Mandy's bringing Dave to the party, but just as arm candy, there's nothing going on.*'

 Usage Note – **eye candy, hot, fit, himbo.**

ASL (*Ay-es-el*) – acronym for age, sex, location. Used to ask someone's vital statistics. Developed from internet chat room conversations, where users come from all across the world, and often fabricate their responses to the question posed by ASL.

As used in the sentence: '*Hi . . . I'm Courtney, what's your ASL?*'

ATM (*Ay-tee-em*) – another internet-derived acronym, this one meaning 'at the moment'.

As used in the sentence: '*ATM I CBA to go out . . . sorry.*'

Bb

Badman *(bah-d-man)* – a rude boy, someone who thinks they are very cool, and dresses in a certain way to prove it. The exact sartorial code, however, depends on the badman's social group.

As used in the sentence: *'Mo's way changed since he moved schools – now he's a badman.'*

—————

Bait *(bay-t)* – (1) something that's obvious.

As used in the conversation: *'This is my new phone.' 'Obv – that's so bait.'*

(2) a term to describe the opposite sex.

As used in the sentence: *'I gotta get me some bait tonight.'*

Banging *(bah-ng-in)* – something that's great, or attractive. Anything that bangs (in the conventional sense, i.e. doors) would not be described as banging in the modern sense unless they were *actually* banging.

As used in the sentence: *'I went clubbing last night – the music was banging and so were the girls.'*

Bare *(b-air)* – very much, a lot of something.

As used in the sentence: *'I ate bare chocolate today, I'm prob gonna get muffin top.'*

▶ Usage Note: **muffin top.**

Beast *(bee-st)* – something that's very cool. Commonly used to congratulate male teens on the acquiring of female teens' attention e.g. 'She likes you . . . you beast!'

As used in the sentence: *'Your trainers are beast man, where did you get dem from?'*

Beef *(bee-f)* – to be extremely annoyed. Beef is also often used to initiate a fight, like saying, 'you wanna take this outside?'

  As used in the sentence: *'Quit looking at my man, ho – I got beef with you.'*

Benny *(beh-nee)* – to become angry and possibly have a tantrum. Often riotous if people called Ben get angry.

  As used in the sentence: *'He missed the bus and had a total benny. What a midiot.'*

 Usage Note: **Midiot.**

BiPod *(by-poh'd)* – to share your MP3 music player (iPod if you are 'down', any other brand if you are 'brassic') with someone.

  As used in the conversation: *'Can we BiPod?' 'No . . . I'm too ShyPod.'*

book 14

Blaps *(blah'ps)* – to attack or hit someone in jest. Or in da chest.

As used in the sentence: *'Shut up now or I'll blaps you hard.'*

Blates *(blay-ts)* – obviously, blatantly. Because using three syllables makes you sound too geeky.

As used in the sentence: *'It's 6–0, the game's over – I won, blates.'*

BOBFOC *(boh'b-fok)* – acroynm for 'Body Off *Baywatch*, Face Off *Crimewatch*.' Which not-so-kindly defines someone with a hot body, but ugly face.

As used in the sentence: *'I was on my way over when she turned around – a total BOBFOC. So I came back to you guys. Gutted – I'd thought I was well in!'*

Book *(booh'k)* – cool. See Page 17.

As used in the sentence: *'Let's go shopping – these clothes are way book.'*

Bovvered *(boh-verd)* – unbothered, uninterested. Popularised by comedienne Catherine Tate's sarcastic catchphrase, 'Am I bovvered?' To which the answer is always, no.

As used in the conversation:

Mother: *'Please remember to take the bin out tonight – if you don't I'll be really angry tomorrow.'*

Son: *'Bovvered.'*

Brap *(brah-p)* – an annoying noise to show appreciation or congratulation.

As used at a sports game: *'brap brap!'*

Brass *(br-ar-z)*– really cold. Originates from the phrase 'cold enough to freeze the balls off a brass monkey'.

As used in the sentence: *'Man alive, it's brass out there!*

Brassic *(br-ar-z-ick)* – lacking in funds or cashola. Old school translation of skint.

As used in the sentence: *'I'm totally brassic this week . . . lends us a note.'*

Breh *(br-air)* – friend, stems from a contraction of 'brethren' and is related to the gang term 'brother' which can also be shortened to 'Bro', and most recently, 'Broseph'.

As used in the sentence: *'Breh, can't believe you're moving – I'm devo.'*

Bromance *(bro-mance)* – a best guy friend. A brotherly romance between two friends, usually platonic.

As used in the sentence: *'Look at those two . . . what a bromance!'*

Bungalowed *(b-un-gah-loh-d)* – extremely drunk. Usually prefixed by 'Totally', 'Utterly' or 'Completely'. No one is ever just plain bungalowed.

As used in the sentence: *'I've totally blanked last night, can't remember anything after 8pm, when I started to get utterly battered. Wait . . . did I already tell you that? I'm still completely bungalowed. LOL.'*

Butters *(buh-turz)* – an extremely ugly person or thing. A dilution of the American phrase 'butt ugly'.

As used in the sentence: *'I keep having nightmares about last night – that girl I pulled was butters.'*

BOOK

Book started to be used in place of the word 'cool' because attempting to type cool, or 2665, in a predictive text message, where a mobile phone tries to guess what word the user is intending to type, brings up the word 'book'. Text language has spawned a wide range of new contexts for old phrases, such as 'nun', for someone's mum, and 5477, 'lips', for – somewhat confusingly – 'kiss'. So a predictive text phrase might read:

Cycle? U good? Book! Lets Fat and get adds at sub? Gr8 new carnage

which would work out as:

Awake? U home? Cool! Lets Eat and get beer at pub? Great new barmaid.

book 18

Sometimes numbers replace letters altogether: if a teenager tells you they 459 you, don't get offended: it means 'I love you'.

In fact, this practice has become so established that even the linguists have got involved. They call the language 'textonyms', or 't9onyms' – pronounced tynonyms – after the abbreviation for predictive text as 'T9' – text on nine keys – in many phones. Of course, if you've only just worked out that :) was a smiley emoticon and not a grammatical mistake, then you've got a lot of catching up to do.

Cc

Caj (*cah-jj*) – a contraction of 'casual', this usually confers agreement and is used in a similar context to 'cool'.

As used in the sentence: *'Shall we bunk games?'* *'Caj, yeah.'*

Cane (*cay-n*) – to feel pain. From the public school word for 'ouch, it wasn't me, Sir'. Possibly.

As used in the conversation: *'How was skiing?'* *'Immense, until the last day – I fell over and my knee's been caning ever since.'*

Carnage (*car-naj)*) – a hangover, the result of getting shitted, bungalowed etc.

As used in the sentence: *'I is feeling like carnage today, and I is looking it too – but last night was def worth it.'*

***

CBA (*see-bee-aye*) – acronym for 'Can't Be Arsed'; feeling lazy.

As used in the conversation: *'You coming out tonight?' 'No, I CBA.'*

***

Chat breeze (to) (*chah-t bree-z*) – to speak rubbish; to discuss nothing in particular.

As used in the sentence: *'I'm not listening to you anymore – what you talking bout? You chatting breeze? You're wasting my time.'*

***

Chav (*chavv*) – Lower-class member of society.

Author's Note: A little subjective, this one, but Chav is generally used to snobbishly describe someone regarded as beneath the speaker. Physical characteristics might include a Burberry cap and tracksuit, accessorised with thick gold Argos-bought jewellery – and one or more Asbos. Might be found driving a Vauxhall C(h)avalier, with a tendency to hang around in tribes.

As used in the sentence: *'Destiny is so chav I can't even believe it – she's even twocced my Burb cap.'*

Chirps (to) *(chur-ps)* – to chat up someone; probably derived from the noise 'birds' (i.e. girls) make when communicating to each other. Imitated by the male to get close to the female, as male birds do.

As used in the sentence: *'Ooh she's nice – I'm gonna chirps her, watch and learn!'*

Clocked *(cloh-ked)* – used as a phrase when something is noticed or understood.

As used in the conversation: *'Did you clock that bird, blad'. 'Ay freel. She is butters.'*

Co-dee *(coe-dee)* – a friend. Stems from the term 'co-dependent' in law suits.

As used in the sentence: *'Mum – this is Dan, my co-dee. We're cotching tonight so stay away from the crib.'*

Cool beans (*cool beens*) – an exclamation of high regard, similar to 'great' but totally obscure. What's cool about beans?

As used in the sentence: '*Your new jacket is immense.*' '*Thanks man, cool beans.*'

Co-pilot (*coh-py-lot*) – person on a night out who agrees to stay (relatively) sober or drug-free in order to help ensure the rest of the group get around safely.

As used in the sentence: '*James is co-piloting tonight, so I'm buying his munch.*'

Cotch/Kotch (to) (*coh-tch*) – to chat, and hang out with friends; publicly loiter.

As used in the sentence: '*Want to cotch at mine tonight? Gotta free house.*'

Cream crackered (*cree-m crak-erd*) – knackered, tired; Lacking the 'Big G' (Energy).

As used in the sentence: '*Last night was hectic! I didn't sleep at all – I'm totally cream crackered now tho.*'

Crew *(cr-oo)* – friends; brothers; close associates; fellow gang members.

As used in the sentence: *'Let's get the crew round – I'm bored of being on me jays.'*

Crib *(cr-ib)* – someone's house; where a baby sleeps. Easily confused from a parent's point of view.

As used in the sentence: *'Let's cotch round at Maya's crib – we're near her hood anyway.'*

Cringe *(cri-nj)* – embarrassing. Usually following something done intentionally by the rents.

As used in the sentence: *'His dad caught us in bed. It was sooooo cringe.'*

Cuz *(cuz)* – a close friend who is like a relative. Similar usage to the widened term 'brother'; of the same tribe or family.

As used in the sentence: *'Cuz – you're da man.'*

Dd

Dark *(dah-rk)* – someone or thing that is horrible or tragic.

   As used in the sentence: *'Sam's brother died over the weekend – it's so dark.'*

Dead that *(ded-thah-t)* – to stop an argument or fight.

   As used in the sentence: *'The teacher's coming, I refuse to spend another afternoon in detention, dead that fight, like now.'*

Deets (*dee-ts*) – details. Why bother with two syllables when you can squeeze a word conveniently down to one? Asking for someone's 'deets' rather than details leaves more time for cotching in front of YouTube or catching some zeds.

As used in the sentence: *'Gimme your deets, yeah? I might wanna take you out some time . . .'*

Devo (*dev-oh*) – mild devastation.

As used in the sentence: *'They've done a Jamie Oliver and taken chips off the canteen menu – I'm devo.'*

Digits (*dij-its*) – phone number. The word 'number' is now as old school as 'address'.

As used in the sentence: *'Gimme your digits and I'll hook you up.'*

Diss (to) (*dis*) – to mock someone or something. Contraction of disrespect and now much more popular than the original term. Diss is a perfect example of modern day culture chopping words in half and thus creating a new one-syllable word.

As used in the sentence: *(1) 'Don't you dare diss me . . .'*

(2) 'I can't believe that punk dissed me like that.'

Diz-zay *(diz-ay)* – to describe something or someone as cool. An upwards lilting of the 'ay' usually drives the point home. Different to being 'dizzy' after a few WKDs.

As used in the sentence: *'The new guys at school are all well diz-zay.'*

DLS *(dee-ell-ess)* – acronym for dirty little secret. Usually gossip that doesn't remain secret for long.

As used in the sentence: *'I'll give you my digits but you should know that I'm actually nineteen . . . but keep that as our DLS, yeah?'*

DND *(dee-enn-dee)* – acronym for 'do not disturb'. Mainly aimed at parents.

As used in the sentence: *'No way you're coming in here, it's totally DND OK?'*

Do *(doo)* – to do someone; to have sex.

　　As used in the sentence: *'He's fit, I'd do him, big style.'*

Dullard *(dull-ard)* – a person who is so boring and dull that they couldn't even be called a twat.

　　As used in the sentence: *'Malcolm is such a massive dullard. A real spod.'*

Douchebag *(doosh-bah-g)* – a lighthearted insult, like describing someone as an idiot. Its origins are far too unpleasant to mention here.

　　As used in the sentence: *'You've spilled water all down me, you massive douchebag.'*

Down *(d-our-n)* – to be part of a group of mates.

　　As used in the sentence: *'I'm down with them – they love me.'*

Dragon, the *(drah-gun)* – bad breath. The dragon is the reason chewing gum stains ruin our pavements.

As used in the sentence: *'Mate, you got any gum? I got the dragon.'*

Drunk dial *(drun-k-die-al)* – phoning or texting someone while under the influence of alcohol and making inappropriate comments.

As used in the sentence: *'I drunk dialled him last night and told him we all thought he was fugly . . . a real butters. Now I have to sit next to him in biology . . . Cringe!'*

 Usage Note: **cringe, butters, fugly.**

Dry *(dr-i)* – something that's tedious or dull.

As used in the sentence: *'Maths was especially dry today – I'm gonna drop it after GCSEs.'*

Duh *(d-uh)*– exclamation to describe something as obvious.

As used in the sentence: *'You're so stunning.' 'Well, duh, I have a mirror – I know I am.'*

DRUNK DIAL

Drunk dialing has gained a lot of media attention in recent years, with newspapers rushing to report on new initiatives enabling mobile users to stop themselves from communicating under the influence of alcohol. Ideas have included users setting up bans on phoning specific numbers at certain times; Google has developed a drunk email protector; and phones are now incorporating breathalyzer functions. But none have really taken off – so far. So expect to hear more mumbled declarations of love, sex and/or desire to do GBH on a voicemail near you in the future.

Ee

Emo *(ee-mow)* – the new type of goth; an angst-ridden teenager who likes music that sounds depressing, usually wears skinny jeans, with long black hair covering the eyes. Can be male or female. Sometimes you can't tell the difference. See Page 96.

As used in the sentence: *'He's an emo. He likes death.'*

Endz *(enn-dzz)* – neighbourhood, or the environs of a gang's territory.

As used in the sentence: *'Don't go there mate – that's the Blues' endz.'*

Ennit *(eh-nit)* – the new-school version of the old-school 'innit'. This generally infers agreement.

As used in the conversation: *'Wanna go down the high street?' 'Ennit.'*

Evil *(ee-vil)* – when this term is used as a noun, in the format 'to give someone an evil', it means a horribly expressive look. Popularised by Matt Lucas's Vicky Pollard in *Little Britain,* whose notable catchphrase 'don't go giving me evils' is said very fast and very frequently.

As used in the sentence: *'It wasn't me that blapped her – so why are you giving me evils?'*

 Usage Note: **blap**

Ex-hole *(ex-hole)* – conflation of the words 'ex' and 'arsehole' to describe an ex-partner who is now despised. One person's ex-hole will normally be referred to in this way by all friends to demonstrate loyalty.

As used in the sentence: *'I can't go to that pub, I might see my ex-hole there and seeing his fugly mug would make me vom.'*

 **FYI**

EYE CANDY

You can never have enough words to describe some-one as attractive or desirable – especially if you are a teenage boy or girl.

Check out just a fraction of the sheer bewildering variety available below:

Bait	Horny
Banging	GILF
Beaut	Lush
Buff	Peng
Eye candy	MILF
Fit	Studly
Fly	Studmuffin
Hotty	Unreal

Ff

Facebook *(f-ace-boo-k)* – as a verb (associated with the social networking website www.facebook.com), it means to scrutinise or check out; stalk.

As used in the sentence: *'I'm gonna Facebook that cow to see where she lives.'*

Fakebook *(fay-k-book)* – used as a verb, this means to set up a fake Facebook account, usually for the purpose of insulting or annoying someone anonymously.

As used in the sentence: *'Courtney made me pissed last night – so I Fakebooked her today and posted some ming photos.'*

Fap (*f-app*) – to be intoxicated. Usually with alcohol.

As used in the sentence: *'No surprises last night – Dan was fapped, we had to take him home at nine – standard . . .'*

Faux mo (*f-oh-mo*) – an effeminate male heterosexual; someone who is well dressed, slightly camp and looks after himself . . . but dates women.

As used in the sentence: *'Mike is such a faux mo. Look at his new manbag!'*

Feel me (*f-eel-mee*) – to understand one's position or sentiment. Can actually also mean to touch; be felt up. Be careful when you make this distinction.

As used in the sentence: *'I want you to help me now, d'ya feel me?'*

Fit (*fi-t*) – adjective to describe someone as attractive, sexy. Derives from approved for an athletic body. Presumably.

As used in the sentence: *'She's well fit – I wanna get me some of that.'*

Flatroofing *(fl-ah-t-roo-fing)* – to work hard. You won't see this that often among the Yoof.

As used in the sentence: *'Can't come out tonight, I'm flatroofing it for my zams.'*

Floss *(floss)* – to show off for the sake of gaining undeserved attention.

As used in the sentence: *'The car? He's just flossing, it's actually his nan's.'*

Folded *(foll-ded)* – very, very drunk. Yet another popular word to suggest intoxication and one that has nothing whatsoever to do with what it describes. Probably used for the first time when drunk and just stuck.

As used in the sentence: *'I'm going home, I'm folded.'*

Fomo *(f-oh-mo)* – acronym meaning fear of missing out. Every teenager's worst nightmare.

As used in the sentence: *'She was tired but Sarah's fomo meant she turned up at the party.'*

Fo' shizzle *(foh-shi-zel)*– phrase meaning definitely, certainly. Derivation of American slang and mutated into something that is total nonsense.

As used in the conversation: *'Wanna come to the cinema tonight?' 'Fo shizzle.'*

Free house *(fr-ee-how-se)* – not a pub, but a home from which parents are absent for the evening or weekend. 'Free house' most definitely means 'Party'.

As used in the conversation: *'Let's get hammered at mine tonight – I've got a free house.'*

Freel *(fur-eel)*– Exclamation. Inferring truth – from the Latin phrase *pro verus* meaning 'For real'.

As used in the conversation: *'Did you just fart in my Lucozade?' 'Ai. Freel.'*

Frenemy *(fr-eh-ne-me)* – someone who is perceived to be a friend but is actually detested.

As used in the sentence: *(1) 'Keep your friends close, but your frenemies even closer.'*
(2) 'He's a right nobber, totally a frenemy.'

Fronting *(fron-tin)* – pretending to be someone else. Someone better usually.

As used in the sentence: *'He was wearing his brother's gear – it was bare fronting.'*

Frosted *(froh-sted)* – someone who is dripping in diamante 'bling'.

As used in the sentence: *'Do you remember that girl from the club who was totally frosted?'*

Fudge *(fuh-dj)* – a complete idiot; numpty; the letters of 'fudge' representing the addressee's supposed A Level/GCSE marks.

As used in the sentence: *'You're such a fudge.'*

Fugly *(fug-lee)* – someone who is really unattractive; a compound of 'fucking' and 'ugly'.

As used in the sentence: *'He made a move on me but he was so fugly, there was no way anything was going to happen.'*

FACEBOOK

Social networking websites have created their own pools of vocabulary, despite their relative youth – Facebook, for example, has only existed since 2003. But now the word Facebook, for example, can also be used as a noun in the form a 'Facebook stalker' – someone who has discovered everything that's going on in your life through Facebook. A 'Facebook whore', meanwhile, is an obsessive Facebook user who will probably spend several unproductive hours a day doing very little on the site. 'Facebook rape' (or Frape) is the act of hacking into a user's account to change information about them, while a 'Facebook friend' is someone who is specifically not a real friend, but more akin to an acquaintance (which is how teenagers have hundreds of 'Facebook friends', while the over-thirties struggle to track down fifty, and that includes accepting at least ten 'friend requests' to unrecognised names).

Twitter, a rival social networking website, has also created new meanings for words – 'tweet', for example, is a message update, while a 'follower' is someone who has logged on to receive another user's information updates. If you already knew that because you spend hours a day on the site, you're not a Twitter whore – you're just suffering from Twitterhoea. Niiice.

Gaff *(gah-f)* – something that is fake, or dodgy-looking. Like a fake tan.

    As used in the sentence: *'Is that watch ganked? It looks gaff.'*

Gank *(gan-k)* – describes the act of stealing, usually referring to an easy crime.

    As used in the sentence: *'I left my bag out in Starbucks and my wallet got ganked – I'm gutted.'*

Gash *(ga-ash)* – to describe something as bad. But not bad as in good. Or bad as in naughty. But bad as in terrible. Confused?

As used in the sentence: *'Today was gash, I shoulda just stayed in bed.'*

Gazeboed *(gah-zee-bowed)* – drunk. Made famous by comedian Michael McIntyre and currently popular among the upper-middle classes. If you're going to use this word in this context, YouTube its history.

As used in the sentence: *'Uuuuggh I could barely get up this morning, I was totally gazeboed last night.'*

Geddit *(ged-it)* – understood. Geddit, a slang contraction of 'I get it', is usually used as a question.

As used in the sentence: *'I'm going to smash your face in if you don't, geddit?'*

Get smashed (to) *(geh-t- sm-ashed)* – to get blind drunk.

As used in the sentence: *'I'm done with flatroofing for zams – let's go out and get smashed, whadya reckon?'*

Goddit (*god-dit*) – a slang contraction of 'I've got it'.

As used in the conversation: *'You're gonna have to pick me up, my car's busted.'* *'Goddit.'*

Gouchy (*gow-chi*) – comfortable or relaxed. Possibly stoned.

As used in the sentence: *'I'm zonked, tonight I'm just gonna sit around at home being gouchy.'*

Grimy (*gry-mee*) – something a teenager thinks is brilliant, but a parent probably won't.

As used in the sentence: *'Matt got us a massive stash of booze, we can pre-game until we're obliterated.'* *'Grimy!'*

Gutted (*guh-ted*) – to be majorly disappointed.

As used in the sentence: *'I put on weight on holiday in Shagaluf – gutted.'*

Gutted city *(guh-ted-ci-tee)* – a term to describe even more extreme feeling of depression.

As used in the sentence: *'He dumped me last week. I was totally shocked and now I'm still in gutted city.'*

GAY

The word gay has become a new-school generic insult meaning 'crap' and/or 'rubbish'. Nowadays, the word is unrelated to its origin as 'carefree' and has even strayed beyond its definitions to sexuality with which it has been associated since the late twentieth century.

The word gay has caused recent media controversy. It is felt that the word's current incarnation associates negatively with the gay and lesbian communities. This is an ongoing issue so refrain from using the word.

> As used in the conversation: *'Your car is so gay.'*
> This might result in the response: *'Your mum.'*

▶ Usage Note: **your mum.**

Hh

Hammered *(hah-mur-d)* – to become verrrrrrrry druuuuuuuuunk, so that it becomes impossible to describe until the next morning, when your head has a thumping headache that makes you feel as if you have been assaulted by a violent hand-holding hammer. AKA hammered.

As used in the sentence: *'Last night I got so hammered, all I can remember is nicking that trolley . . . Standard.'*

Heavy *(heh-vee)* – cool. Originated in the 60s to describe something that was serious. Now it can mean anything that is remotely interesting.

As used in the sentence: *'Shanice in* Big Brother *was acting well heavy last night!'*

Hench *(hen-ch)* – describes someone as big; muscular; a brick shithouse.

As used in the sentence: *'I've been at the gym non-stop, check these guns out – I'm getting really hench.'*

Himbo *(him-boh)* – yes, bimbo has crossed the sexual divide and a himbo is now used to describe a hot male who is thicker than a plank of wood.

As used in the sentence: *'He was hot, but too much of a himbo. I need someone clever enough to chat about 24 with me – but he was just nowhere near that level.'*

Homies *(ho-mees)* – friends; mates or fellow gang members. Has travelled across the pond following the contraction of the US term 'homeboy'.

As used in the sentence: *'I'm vexed with my homies – can I grab some munch with you instead?'*

Hood *(hoodd)* – home area, neighbourhood, local place to loiter.

As used in the sentence: *'I'm cream crackered and CBA to go out but I do wanna see you – come cotch in my hood?'*

Hooked up *(hoo-ked-up)* – started a new relationship.

As used in the sentence: *'Annie and Dave have finally hooked up – it's so cute.'*

Hot *(h-ot)* – attractive.

As used in the sentence: *'Kelly's new boyf is ming, it's so weird coz she's well hot.'*

Hush your gums *(hu-sh-yor-guh-ms)* – be quiet; keep schtum.

As used in the sentence: *'I've got a headache, hush your gums!'*

Ii

Ice *(eye-suh)* – diamonds, flashy jewellery and bling.

As used in the sentence: *'This Valentine's Day, I'm gonna buy her some ice coz I'm actually really into her.'*

Ick *(ii-k)* – something really unpleasant, nasty, disgusting.

As used in the sentence: *'Ick . . . Your piercing's gone septic!'*

Ignoranus *(ig-nor-ay-nus)* – a massive idiot. A play on the word ignoramus which commonly denotes ignorance and/or stupidity.

As used in the sentence: *'You're a total ignoranus.'*

IMHO *(aye-em-atch-oh)* – internet-derived acronym for 'In My Humble Opinion'.

As used in the sentence: *'You're a minging douchebag. IMHO.'*

IM-ing *(eye-em-ing)* – participating in instant messaging (that's a conversation on the internet via software, such as MSN Messenger, Google Chat or Skype Chat, which mainly uses typed words to 'compunicate'). The rapidity of response required in IM-ing has initiated a deluge of shortened words and acronyms – see, for example, IMHO, CBA, JW, LOL, LMAO, IMHO, ATM . . .

As used in the sentence: *'I'm IM-ing Steve so I'll Facebook you later.'*

Innit *(inn-it)* – to agree; has rapidly replaced the word 'yes', and can be found spoken by both middle and upper class people.

As used in the conversation: *'You want to eat munch at mine?' 'Innit.'*

Insane *(inn-sane)* – ridiculous and/or pointless.

As used in the sentence: *'It's kind of insane but I'm gonna cut.'*

Ish *(ii-sh)* – can mean moderate, a bit; used as an alternative to ambivalent.

As used in the sentence: *'I'm thinking of going to see Rob in France but I'm not sure – he's a bit ish about it.'*

Itching *(it-ching)* – to want something very much; to crave – as in to want to scratch an itch so bad. Can also refer to this literally (see (2)).

As used in the sentence: *(1) 'She's itching to come visit me in France but I haven't told her that I've got me a new girl out here...'*

(2) 'I can't believe Shanice has nits . . . she's itching all over the shop.'

IRRITAINMENT

Irritainment is the new form of very light (see-through, actually) entertainment that's addictive and trashy and that even the watcher realises is pretty bad. Irritainment is best summed up by *The Jeremy Kyle Show* and, of course, *Big Brother*, but most people have their own secret addictions to some kind of irritainment be it *Pimp My Ride* (on MTV), *Hole in the Wall* (BBC) or *Hollyoaks* (Channel 4).

As used in the sentence: '*I know* Extreme Makeover *is complete irritainment, but I'm hooked.*'

Jack (to) *(jah-ck)* – steal, most often used in the past tense as 'jacked' for stolen.

As used in the sentence: *'Facebook me– don't call. Milton jacked me phone last night – I'm in a total benny.'*

Jail bait *(j-ayle-bay-t)* – someone who is under the age of sexual consent.

As used in the sentence: *'Stay away dude – she's jail bait.'*

Jam *(j-ah-m)* – to meet with friends; relax; hang out; veg.

As used in the sentence: *'We're going to jam, you wanna come?'*

Jargonaut *(j-arr-go-nawt)* – someone who uses way too much jargon in their vocabulary. Or over-pimps it, one could say.

As used in the sentence: *'Mike's dad got some book called* Pimp Your Vocab *and now he's like a total jargonaut – massive cringe.'*

 Usage Note: **massive cringe, pimp.**

Jeeeeez *(jee-yz)* – contraction of 'Jesus', used as a general exclamation – like 'aah' – to express surprise, shock, or disgust. Identify which by checking out the context – someone who says 'jeeeeez' after falling into a man-hole full of sewage probably doesn't mean 'hooray!'

As used in the sentence: *'You wanna borrow my GHDs? Jeeeez, girl, no way is that gonna happen!'*

Jel *(j-ell)* – envious, a contraction of 'jealous'.

As used in the sentence: *'Sweet!, You got that much cash? I'm jel.'*

Jiggy *(jig-ee)* – (1) adjective to describe something that looks good.

As used in the sentence: *'Mandy looks jiggy – I'm well pissed off I dumped her.'*

(2) a loose reference to sexual activity.

As used in the sentence: *'Tonight's the night we're gonna get jiggy.'*

Jog on *(joh-g-ohn)* – walk on or go away, can also be used to mean 'no way' – as in, 'take a hike'.

As used in the sentence: *'Jog on, man – nothing to see.'*

Jokes *(joe-ks)* – to have a good time.

As used in the sentence: *'We all went shopping, it was absolute jokes.'*

Jook *(jew-ks)* – confusingly this can refer to the act of stabbing or stealing. Try taking in a bit of context to work out which is being referred to.

As used in the sentence: *'My bling was all jooked last week and I CBA to replace it until I get more pee.'*

JSYK *(jay-es-why-kay)* – another acronym, this time for 'just so you know'. Used interchangeably with 'FYI'.

As used in the sentence: *'JSYK, Imogen's not coming to the beach – think she's scared of exposing her muffin top, but she says her rents won't let her.*

Juiced *(joo-st)* – to be excited about something or someone.

As used in the sentence: *'It's nearly the holidays – I'm juiced!'*

JW *(j-double-you)* – internet-derived acronym for 'just wondering/just wondered'.

As used in the conversation: *'Why did you wanna know bout my ice?' 'JW.'*

Kk

K *(kay)* – the new 'OK' – Teenglish is often keen to abbreviate where possible. Where 'K' is used there's often a feeling of apathy involved – it usually indicates less than full-hearted agreement.

As used in the conversation: *'Wanna help me collect dust particles for my latest experiment?' 'Umm.. K...'*

Kaka *(car-car)* – used as a noun to mean 'shit', usually referring to a horrible object or deed.

As used in the sentence: *'I can't believe you did that to me – you are such a kaka.'*

Kapeesh *(ca-peesh)* – to understand, usually used as a question. Derives from the Italian 'capisci' (do you understand?) and rose to prominence through the success of the *Godfather* trilogy which many male teens relate to (and replicate) through mob-mentality, violence and love of all things mafia-esque – guns, drugs and shooting people. The word has remained fixed to its original definition but has taken on a lot harsher context.

As used in the sentence: *'Get out of my face . . . Kapeesh?'*

Keeno *(key-no)* – someone who is fanatical about something.

As used in the sentence: *'Ever since Wimbledon he's been obsessed with tennis – he won't even come out with me to jack some wallets – he's turned into a keeno. It's lame.'*

Kerching *(ker-ching)* – used as an onomatopoeic exclamation to mean 'in the money', although often used sarcastically too.

As used in the sentence: *'Claire's rents pay her £3 an hour to babysit . . . and they think that's kerching. It's total slavery.'*

Kick arse (to) *(kik-arr-se)* – to succeed or do very well at something, e.g. win a sports event.

As used in the sentence: *'It finished at 4–0, we kicked arse.'*

Kicking *(k-ick-ing)* – a term of approval, like great, awshum and banging.

As used in the sentence: *'The club was kicking – had an immense time.'*

Kick it *(k-ick-it)* – to relax and hang out somewhere.

As used in the sentence: *'Let's kick it at mine tonight – the rents are away.'*

Kneecap *(nee-cap)* – to ruin someone's reputation in an especially nasty way. A kneecapper is someone who carries out the act of kneecapping.

As used in the sentence: *'Everyone knows about Andy's problems down below now – Katy totally kneecapped him.'*

Knob *(noh-b)* – a knob is an idiot. And vice versa.
   As used in the sentence: *'You're such a knob!*

 Usage Note: **midiot.**

Knobber *(noh-berr)* – a more affectionate term, this is nonetheless used to describe an idiot.
   As used in the sentence: *'You ate my last bit of chocolate? You're such a knobber!'*

Krank *(krah-nk)* – deeply uncool.
   As used in the sentence: *'Your dad is krank.'*

Labatyd *(lah-ba-tide)* – a sarcastic riposte akin to 'my heart bleeds', labatyd stands for 'Life's a bitch and then you die'.

As used in the conversation: *'I left my iPod on the Tube.'*

'Yeah, well, labatyd.'

Label whore *(lay-bell-haw)* – someone who only wears brand-name clothes.

As used in the sentence: *'You're such a label whore.'*

Lame *(lay-mmm)* – sad, uncool. This word had been around for decades but then disappeared. It has returned in the last few years and now become even more popular.

As used in the conversation: *'I'm flatroofing tonight, not coming out on the lash.' 'Serious? You're so lame.'*

Lash *(lah-sh)* – (1) to borrow something from somebody.

As used in the sentence: *'Lash me a tenner?'*

(2) to describe the process of getting drunk.

As used in the sentence: *'Wanna come out tonight? We're gonna get lashed.'*

Lay out (to) *(lay-owt- to)* – to spend money frivously.

As used in the sentence: *'It's a lot of dosh but I love it – I'm gonna lay out.'*

Ledge *(leh-dj)* – way of describing someone who is cool, contraction of 'legend'.

As used in the sentence: *'Mate, you're a ledge for letting me gank your homework.'*

Let's bounce *(leh-ts-bow-nce)* – let's get out of here.

As used in the sentence: *'I'm done with this hood – let's bounce.'*

Lights are on *(lye-ts-ar-on)* – code for 'parents are in the room'.

As used in the sentence: *'JSYK, lights are on . . .'*

'lo *(low)* – greeting, contraction of hello.

As used in the sentence: *"lo. Sup? You got any artichokes?'*

▶ Usage Note: **sup.**

LOL *(ell-oh-ell)* – (1) acronym for 'laugh out loud' to describe something that's very funny.

As used in the sentence: *'Hilarious, that was totally LOL.'*

(2) (more usually in a written context, such as a text message) acronym for 'lots of love'.

As used in the sentence: *'ty for ur help babe, lol x'*

Long *(lon-g)* – someone or something that is being annoying, usually for causing a lot of effort.

As used in the sentence: *'I told him he was being long because he wouldn't come and see me.'*

Lush *(luh-sh)* – very nice. After becoming very passé in the 1990's, Lush has returned with a vengeance.

As used in the sentence: *'Mmm . . . That guy is lush.'*

LIKE

The word 'Like' is such a pervasive part of Teenglish that it has become meaningless. It often used to mean 'said' but nowadays it is predominantly used as a senseless sentence filler to bridge words where 'um', 'erm' and 'ah' used to work just as well.

As used in the sentence: *'Like, I said that he, like, wanted to go out yeah, but, like, he never, like, called me back so I'm like, man, waiting and, you know, whatever, fed up an' stuff, like, god, he's such a jerk like.'*

When 'like' is used in a context that seems similar to its more traditional referent – to get on with someone – it will normally mean a romantic rather than benign attachment.

As used in the sentence: *'So I was like, whatevs, and she was like, yeah but like I CBA, and then she said she liked him.'*

Mm

Malt *(mahlt)* – a bizarre term to describe a girlfriend, usually inferred with negative connotations. Nothing to do with a chocolate milkshake additive.

As used in the sentence: *'Man, is that your malt? Has she got muffin top?!'*

Man alive *(mah-n-ah-live)* – exclamation of incredulity.

As used in the sentence: *'Man alive – he's ming!'*

Manor *(man-or)* – the area where someone lives, or often a specific reference to someone's house. Denotes an ironic sense of delusion.

As used in the sentence: *'Are you coming round my manor?'*

Mardy *(marr-dee)* – grumpy, in a mood.

As used in the sentence: *'Ignore Rachel – she's in a mardy because no one remembered it's the anniversary of her getting her belly pierced.'*

Mare *(may-r)* – a nightmare. Not to be confused with a female horse over the age of three.

As used in the sentence: *'My computer crashed, I lost all my work – it was a total mare. And my teachers don't believe me.'*

Marinating *(mah-rin-ate-ing)* – hanging out, chilling and relaxing.

As used in the sentence: *'Let's marinate in your crib coz it's gonna be heavy later.'*

Mash up *(mah-sh-up)* – mixing stuff together, usually used in the context of music.

As used in the sentence: *'I made you this playlist for your iPod – it's a mash up of my fave songs, so obv it's immense.'*

Massive cringe *(mah-siv-cri-nj)* – really embarrassing. Note that 'massive' in general is like 'immense' – a popular generic adjective.

As used in the conversation: *'You've got a bogey hanging down your face.' 'Oh, massive cringe!'*

McPee *(muc-pee)* – to go to use a toilet in a restaurant, bar, hotel etc. without paying for the privilege of doing so.

As used in the sentence: *'I'm desperate, I'm going to do a McPee.'*

Midiot *(mi-dee-ot)* – fusing of 'massive' and 'idiot' to describe someone as a 'massive idiot'. Generally used in an affectionate rather than malicious manner.

As used in the conversation: *'Mum, you're being a midiot!'*

'What's that, dear, a middle idiot?'

'NO! A massive idiot – and what you just said proves it!'

MILF (*mill-fff*) – an attractive older woman. This is an acronym for 'mother I'd like (to) fuck'. Popularised in the cult teen film *American Pie*, famous examples might include Demi Moore and Jade Jagger.

As used in the sentence: *'Chris thinks Kate's mum's a proper MILF.'*

Ming (*min-g*) – to describe something or someone as horrible, ugly or disgusting.

As used in the sentence: *'Ugh, I just stepped in . . . ugh, what is that? It stinks . . . that's so ming.'*

Minger *(min-ger)* – to refer to a person as ugly but who is not quite a 'fugly pug'.

As used in the sentence: *'Something totally devo happened to me yesterday . . . I pulled this girl and when the lights went on I realised she was a right minger.'*

Minging *(min-ging)* – ugly. Not as nasty as fugly, pugly or rank.

As used in the conversation: *'My skin is minging at the mo – these spots are insane!'*

Mint *(min-t)* – to describe something as exceptional.

As used in the sentence: *'Danielle won the lottery – mint!*

Mob – *(moh'b)* contraction of mobile phone.

As used in the sentence: *'Gimme my mob back – I got no pee on it.'*

Moob *(moo-b)* – a 'man boob' – or in a more general context, a top heavy man.

As used in the sentence: *'I'm not going swimming till I've got rid of my moobs, otherwise everyone will take the piss out of me.'*

Muffin top *(muh-fin-toh-p)* – the spread of fat when someone wears too-tight trousers so their stomach bulges out. Like the top of a muffin bulging out of its casing . . .

As used in the sentence: *'Ugh, she wore her skinnies and had total muffin top – it made me wanna vom.'*

Mug *(muh-g)* – (1) noun, an idiot, someone who is easily exploitable/vunerable.

As used in the sentence: *'I left my gear at Amanda's – I feel like a right mug.'*

(2) verb, to give someone a dirty stare.

As used in the sentence: *'Are you mugging me? You got beef?'*

Munch *(muh-nch)* – a snack. Coined after the onomatapeic sound made when eating – a much more modern version of the extremely popular word 'food'.

As used in the sentence: *'I'm starving, let's get some munch.'*

Museum foot *(mew-see-um-fut)* – feeling tired and bored. Refers to the feeling some might report after walking around a museum for a long time.

As used in the sentence: *'I was rinsed by that shopping trip . . . I used up all my pee and now I've got museum foot.'*

My bad *(mi-ba-d)* – a mistake. *Mea Culpa.*

As used in the sentence: *'Whoops, soz – that was my bad.'*

Nn

Nang *(nan-g)* – cool, trendy.

　　As used in the sentence: *'This top is nang, I'm gonna buy it.'*

Narc *(nah-rk)* – used as a verb to describe falling asleep in an inappropriate situation – derived from the sleeping disorder narcolepsy.

　　As used in the sentence: *'I narced in maths today – Gibson went apeshit.'*

Neek *(nee-k)* – a hybrid of nerd and geek.

As used in the sentence: *'He's babysitting? Your boyf is a total neek.'*

Neeky *(nee-key)* to describe the behaviour of a neek – means out-of-fashion, uncool or sad.

As used in the sentence: *'He was being so bare neeky that I left him and came here.'*

 Usage Note: **bare.**

Nim nim nim *(nih-m-nih-m-nih-m)* – et cetera, like saying 'blah blah blah'.

As used in the context: (teacher): *'And so Pythagoras' theorum is truly the most exciting formula to use in this equation . . .'*

(one student to another) *'Nim nim nim, I'm bored.'*

No brainer *(noh-bray-ner)* – originally meaning something that requires only a very low IQ to understand, this phrase is now more usually applied to questions or decisions with an obvious answer.

As used in the sentence: *'It's a total no brainer – course I'm gonna bunk chemistry to come to meet you.'*

Noob *(noo-b)* – a beginner, novice. Comes from the term 'newbie', often used in internet forums. Do not confuse with 'moob'.

As used in the sentence: *'That was you chirping? Lame – you're such a noob.'*

Nuff *(nu-uff)* – a lot of something, a similar meaning to 'bare'.

As used in the sentence: *'Mate, I got nuff stash for the both of us.'*

Numpty *(nuh-m-ptee)* – an affectionate term to refer to an idiot. Children may refer to parents/teachers/people of authority as numpties without fear of recrimination.

As used in the sentence: *'You expect me to believe that? Ha – you numpty!'*

Obliterated *(oh-bli-ter-ay-ted)* – (1) Very drunk.

As used in the sentence: *'Shousadasldf . . . asdfhsadld . . . caaaaan't speeeeeak . . . obbbbbliiiiterated- dddddddd.'*

(2) Soundly beaten.

As used in the sentence: *'That race was ridiculously long – it's obliterated me.'*

Obv *(ob-v)* – obvious, obviously.

As used in the conversation: *'You know maths is cancelled because Mrs Grant turned up to school off her face?' 'Yeah, obv. Everyone knows that.'*

Off the chain *(off-ther-chay-n)* – very cool. Totally wicked.

As used in the sentence: *'You got the new iPhone? Immense – that's off the chain.'*

Off the hook *(off-ther-hoo-k)* – phrase to describe something that is amazing, fun.

As used in the sentence: *'We're like going to Ibiza this summer – it's gonna be off the hook!'*

Ohnosecond *(oh-no-sec-on-d)* – the feeling of immediate panic after making a big mistake. This phrase derives from the exclamation 'oh, no' that probably coincides with the mistake.

As used in the sentence: *'After drunk dialling and then sending that text to my ex, I had a major ohnosecond.'*

 Usage Note: **drunk dialling.**

OMG *(oh-em-gee)* – acronym referring to the expression Oh My God.

As used in the sentence: *'OMG!! I've run over a pigeon!'*

 Usage Note: **zams.**

On a(nother) level *(on-a-lev-ell)* – used to describe something as extreme, far out.

As used in the sentence: *'It was jokes, like on another level.'*

On it (to be) *(ohn-it)* – to be interested in doing or feeling something.

As used in the sentence: *'You wanna go to the cinema?' 'Yeah for def, I'm so on it.'*

Owned *(oh-wned)* – to be humiliated or embarrassed. The definition is also true of the terms 'boyed' and 'rinsed'.

As used in the sentence: *'Doug gave me a wedgie in the pool, I was massively owned.'*

Pp

Papers *(pay-per-s)* – money, cash (cashola).

As used in the sentence: *'I got enough papers to get us to Oxford Street, but you're gonna have to shell out for lunch.'*

Pedo piff *(pee-doh-pif)* – a girl who is hot/fit/attractive, but much younger than she looks.

As used in the conversation: *'She's hot – I'm going to make a move.'*

'Aw, no don't do it, she's pedo piff.'

Pee *(peee)* – money, cash, coinage.

As used in the sentence: *'Breh, I need that pee back, yeah and don't get pissy with me.'*

Peeps *(pee-ps)* – close friends. Can often refer to relatives.

As used in the sentence: *'I'm a bit CBA about my birthday this year– just gonna invite my peeps for some munch.'*

Peng *(pen-g)* – describes someone who is good-looking, fit, handsome or hot.

As used in the sentence: *'She's peng . . . and not outta my league either.'*

Piff *(pih-f)* – good, often better than something else. (Although the word can also refer to cannabis.)

As used in the sentence: *'I got me these new tunes – and the stuff is straight piff.'*

▶ Usage Note: **tunes.**

Pimp *(pim-p)* – as a verb, to improve something.

As used in the sentence: *'I've pimped my vocab, it's immense.'*

Pinky *(pin-key)* – a fifty-pound note. Because it's reddish.

As used in the conversation: *'Lend me a pinky?' 'Why, you think I got bare?'*

Piss around *(piss-ah-rownd)* – to muck around, waste time, be unproductive.

As used in the sentence: *'Sorry I'm late, I pissed around on YouTube for ages.'*

Pissy *(piss-ee)* – annoying; to be annoyed and get testy (testes).

As used in the sentence: *'Man, you're making me pissy – you better leave now.'*

▶ Usage Note: **Testes**

Player *(play-err)* – someone with a reputation for dating a lot of people, often more than one person at a time.

As used in the sentence: *'Stay away from that guy – he's a player.'*

Pre-game *(pree-gay-m)* – a period of drinking alcohol at someone's home or another cheap location before then going out to a more expensive bar or club.

As used in the sentence: *'I'm skint – but I wanna get bladdered. Come round to mine and we'll pre-game, yeah?'*

Pugly *(pug-lee)* – a very ugly person. Basically a combination of Pig and Ugly.

As used in the sentence: *'I pulled some chick last night – she was so pugly – it was just 'cos I was pissed!'.'*

Quag *(kw-ag)* – problem.

    As used in the sentence: *'What the hell is his quag?*
He's in a total benny.'

 Usage Note: **benny.**

Quality *(kwa-lit-ee)* – adjective to describe something
as fun, great.

    As used in the sentence: *'The gig was quality – you*
missed out.'

83 raw

Rr

Rah *(Ra)* – someone who is posh; a derivation of 'Hoorah Henry'. Often found wearing clothes from Abercrombie & Fitch, or Jack Wills, or wearing a salmon-coloured jumper tied around his or her neck.

As used in the sentence: *'I don't wanna go to that uni, it's totally full of rahs.'*

Raw *(ro – or)* bad or upsetting. A feeling of being left emotionally vulnerable.

As used in the sentence: *'I was bare shocked by that talk – it was raw.'*

Random *(ran-dom)* – used to describe something that was unexpected. Can also explain moments of vagueness.

As used in the sentence: *'He said he loved me, it was so random.'*

Randomer (ran-dom-er) – a stranger; someone who is outside of a social group.

As used in the sentence: *'That guy? I don't know who he is – just some randomer.'*

Raped *(ray-p'd)* – to be beaten by a task or event. This usage of the word rape has spread across the playgrounds and schools like wildfire. A rather unpleasant evolution of a word, flung about without consequence for context.

As used in the sentence: *'That zam was ridiculously hard – question three raped me.'*

Rat arsed *(rat-r-sed)* – yet another term for drunk. Its origins are unknown as rats aren't known to be big drinkers.

As used in the sentence: *'Ugh! I feel rat arsed.'*

Reax *(re-axe)* – abbreviated phrase for 'reaction'.

As used in the sentence: *'He got banged up for the night when the police found him yesterday – his rents are going to go mental in reax.'*

Rents *(rentz)* – an abbreviation of parents, bypassed via Parental Units. Generally used by the very kids who live with you rent-free.

As used in the sentence: *'Come cotch at mine, the rents are away all weekend.'*

Rep *(rep)* – to praise someone's actions; comes from the act of adding to someone's reputation in online forums.

As used in the sentence: *'Thanks for your help, I'll give you rep.'*

Ridonkulous *(re-donc-u-louse)* – to describe something as even more stupid than the word ridiculous would infer (but possibly not as ridiculous as the word 'ridonkulous').

As used in the sentence: *'You're asking me to clean my room when you can see that* Lost *is on? You're being ridonkulous – piss off.'*

Rinsed *(rins-ed)* – (1) adj, overused.

As used in the sentence: *'I'm so over MySpace, it's totally rinsed.'*

(2) verb, embarrassment or humiliation.

As used in the sentence: *'Everyone thought you'd thrash Dan at penalties – but you got rinsed!'*

Rock *(roc)* – adjective to describe something or someone being great. Shortened from the phrase, 'you rock my world'.

As used in the sentence: *'You were amazing last night – thanks for all your help, you rock.'*

Rough *(ru– uff)* – a negative reference to someone's appearance, often used in relation to the morning after the night before, but can refer to general unattractiveness.

As used in the sentence: *'Jeeez you must have had a big one last night – you is looking rough!'*

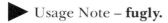 Usage Note – **fugly.**

Safe *(say-f)* – akin to 'cool'.

As used in the conversation: *'Wanna come get some munch at mine?' 'Yeah, safe.'*

Screwed *(skru-w'd)* – in trouble.

As used in the sentence: *'I haven't done my homework, I'm screwed.'*

Screwing *(skru-win)* – (1), *verb,* to describe someone as angry.

As used in the sentence: *'When Mr Jones realised none of us had listened to the whole lesson he started screwing.'*

(2) *adj,* meaning cool.

As used in the sentence: *'That's so screwing!'*

Sesh *(seh-sh)* – a shortened form of the word 'session', usually used to describe a trip or activity.

As used in the sentence: *'After Biology finishes I'm going on a massive boozing sesh!'*

Shagaluf *(shagga–loof)* – A hilarious renaming of a popular Spanish holiday destination for British teens reflecting why British teens go there every summer in droves.

As used in the sentence: *'I'm off to Shagaluf with the crew on Friday. Gonna get me some!'*

Shell out *(sheh-ll ow-t)* – pay for. Usually has negative connotations.

As used in the sentence: *'I gotta shell out for new threads – well annoying.'*

▶ Usage Note: **threads, well**.

Shitfaced *(shit-f-ace'd)* – one of the most common, and popular, adjectives to announce intoxication.
As used in the sentence: *'Get in the first round, I wanna get shitfaced.'*

Shizzle *(shis-el)* – stuff, belongings, property belonging to speaker.
As used in the sentence: *'Get your shizzle together, we're leaving.'*

Shot that *(sh-ot-tha-t)* – get rid of something; a pointless endeavour.
As used in the sentence: *'My uni applications? No – I shot that, it was way boring.'*

Shrapnel *(pay-per-s)* – coins, small amount of money or funds, sometimes referred to as coinage.

As used in the sentence: *'I only got shrapnel left . . . only enough for some rizzlas.'*

Shunting *(shun-ting)* – posing, showing off, flaunting your wares publicly.

As used in the sentence: *'Stop shunting, you're vexing me.'*

Shypod *(sh-aye-poh'd)* – being too embarrassed to show someone your list of saved music on your MP3 player – usually an iPod.

As used in the sentence: *'I wanted to see his music, but he was shyPod. When I grabbed his player I found out why – he had 'Barbie Girl' on his most listened – LMAO!'*

Sick/sik *(sih-k)* – incredible or cool.

As used in the sentence: *'James' parents are sick, they didn't even screw when the neighbours came to whinge that we'd flooded the garden.'*

Sick times *(sih-k-ty-ms)* – fun events or occasions.

As used in the sentence: *'I was thinking about that time we pranked her – sick.'*

Skankaroo *(skah-nk-ah-roo)* – revolting or disgusting. Can be abbreviated to skank, or skanky.

As used in the sentence: *'Your kit is so skankaroo it's offending my eyes.'*

Skett *(skeh-t)* – a (usually female) person who behaves promiscuously and is earmarked as a slut.

As used in the sentence: *'She's such a skett – that's her third guy tonight.'*

Smacked it *(smah-k'd-it)* – to have succeeded or achieved something (or someone).

As used in the sentence: *'I'm not bovvered, I smacked that test.'*

Snap *(snah-p)* – school lunch. Predominantly used by college/sixth form students who now consider themselves as adults and not pupils.

As used in the sentence: *'Lets get some snap before all the babies get out of class.'*

Soontimes *(soon-tye-ms)* – not long, or, indeed, sometime soon.

As used in the sentence: *'When are you gonna pass your driving test?' 'Soontimes, mate.'*

Soz *(soh'z)* – shortened form of 'sorry'.

As used in the sentence: *'Soz, I didn't see you there.'*

Spill *(spi-ll)* – divulge. Contraction from the phrase 'spill the beans'.

As used in the sentence: *'So, how was last night? Spill!'.*

Spod *(spod)* – a nerd; a geek; a dullard. Somebody who is boring and lame. Chances are if you don't know what a spod is then you probably are one.

As used in the sentence: *'Stop being a spod!'*

Standard *(stan-dar'd)* – a popular response to something that is normal, assumed.

As used in the sentence: *'England lost on penalties – standard.'*

Street *(stre– eet)* – referring to teenage culture – from the 'streets', originally relating to underground, gangster terms and behaviour.

As used in the sentence: *'You're lookin bare street today.'*

Sucked *(suk'd)* – verb to describe something as stolen.

As used in the sentence: *'I was sucked last week, still waiting on a new phone.'*

Sup *(su-up)* – a generic greeting, shortened form of 'what's up?'

As used in the sentence: *'Sup kids – got a quag?'*

Swipeout *(swy-p-owt)* – when your cash cards stop working.

As used in the sentence: *'I was about to pay for your present when I realised I'd hit a swipeout . . . So I didn't get you anything. Soz.'*

SOCIAL GROUPS

Social groupings such as emos forge further distinctive neologisms. Emo, for example, has spawned 'emospeak', which is when someone types on web forums, blogs etc. without spaces. As used in the sentence: thisisemospeakitisannoyingtoread.

'Emortant', meanwhile, describes something that is important to an emo group, as used in the sentence, 'That new tune is so emortant'. Or how about 'emovamp' – that's an emotional vampire, which is basically an extreme emo.

As used in the sentence, *'Nathanial's become an emovamp – it's so freaky.'*

TBH *(tee-bee-aitch)* – acronym for 'to be honest'.

    As used in the sentence: *'TBH I really don't want you to do that.'*

Teek – (tee'qu) very old, as in antique.

    As used in the sentence: *'Man alive, that mob is teek.'*

Tell over *(teh'll-oh-ver)* – to be a tell tale, gossip.

As used in the sentence: *'Yeah, so I cheated, whatevs, it was no big deal, just a GCSE – but she told over me, and that's totally not on.'*

 Usage Note: **whatevs.**

Testes *(tess-tease)* – to get angry. Has origins in testy and too good to not change to testes. Obv.

As used in the sentence: *'I'm getting testes now!'*

Threads *(threh-ds)* – clothes. Usually spoken by a Label whore (see page 61)

As used in the sentence: *'Mum, I need new threads, like now.'*

Tight *(ty-t)* – to describe someone as familiar and friendly.

As used in the sentence: *'This is my best friend, we're tight.'*

Toast *(toe'st)* – finished, destroyed.

As used in the sentence: *'I got completely soaked yesterday, it was pissing down – my trainers are toast.'*

Tonk *(t-on-k)* – adjective to describe someone as fit or good-looking.

As used in the sentence: *'He's really tonk.'*

Totally *(toe-tal-ee)* – (1) a filler term which is almost as popular as 'like' amongst some female teens.

As used in the sentence: *'I was totally gonna come to your party, but then I totally forgot. Total nightmare. Sorry!'*

(2) 'of course'.

As used in the sentence: *'I, like, love your hair like that – can you show me how to do it?' 'Totally!'*

Trendies *(tren-dee-s)* – a social tribe, identified by their desire to follow fashion and hanging out in big gangs.

As used in the sentence: *'I went out to get trollied with Emma last night but the place was full of trendies.'*

Tunes *(too-ns)* – music, songs. The word 'song' has been replaced rapidly by 'toons', 'MP3s' and 'downloads'

As used in the sentence: *'Check out my tunes – much better than yours, you numpty.'*

Twoc *(twoh-k)* – acronym for 'take without consent'.

As used in the sentence: *'I woke up in my room, lying on top of this road sign that I twoced last night – I have no idea why, I was totally hammered.'*

Twonk *(twoh-nk)* – an idiot. A mishmash of favoured insults twit, twat and plonker.

As used in the sentence: *'You're such a twonk – I can't believe you just said that.'*

Uu

Uber *(ooh-ber)* – very, or extremely. A German term that crossed over very easily and has become increasingly popular.

As used in the sentence: *'This bar is uber cool.'*

Unass *(unn-ar-se)* – to leave somewhere very fast. As in, to quickly remove one's ass [US for 'arse'] quickly from a place.

As used in the sentence: *'We had to unass when the police arrived.'*

UnGoogleable *(un-goo-gla-bull)* – orginally this meant someone whose name did not come up on a Google search but it has now extended to refer to someone of little importance to a particular topic or social grouping.

As used in the sentence: *'Don't worry 'bout him, he's unGoogleable, no one will take the noise seriously.'*

Unreal *(uh-n-ree-al)* – something amazing or attractive or an unusual looking person. A potential Twonk.

As used in the sentence: *'We were shocked when we met him – he was so immense, it was unreal.'*

Up shit creek *(upp– shih–t- cree-k)* – in big trouble; a contracted form of the phrase 'up shit creek without a paddle'.

As used in the sentence: *'I knew when I saw how hench he was that we were up shit creek.*

 Usage Note: **hench.**

Up the duff *(upp-ther-duh-ff)* – originally referring to pregnancy, this is now used to denote an unfortunate situation.

As used in the conversation: *'Doug's rents are moving to Leeds, he's gotta go too. He's proper up the duff.'*

Vamoosh *(vah-moosh)* – to go.
　　As used in the sentence: *'I'm ready, let's vamoosh.'*

Vamping *(vam-ping)* – showing off.
　　As used in the sentence: *'She was going on and on about all her new shizzle, it was obv vamping.'*

▶ Usage Note: **obv, shizzle.**

Veg *(vedge)* – to relax so much that one lapses into a vegetated state; super chilled.

As used in the sentence: *'Gonna do nothing tonight, just sit at home and veg'*

Vent *(vehn-t)* – to scream, shout, express annoyance. Derived from the phrase 'to vent one's anger'.

As used in the sentence: *'If you don't fix my computer right now I'm gonna vent.'*

Vexing *(vecks-in)* – annoying, upsetting, pissing off.

As used in the sentence: *'Quit vexing me, man. I'm tryin' to watch* Antiques Roadshow.*'*

Vom *(voh-m)* – to vomit, throw up, be sick. But not *that* sick (as in cool).

As used in the sentence: *'His cooking was so gross I wanted to vom – but he was really hot so I pretended it was nice, and later we hooked up.'*

Wagwan *(wog–won)* – what's going on? A greeting, stemming from the Jamaican patois 'wah gwaan'.
   As used in the conversation: *'Sup guys, wagwan.'*

Wannabe *(wuh-nuh-bee)* – someone who tries hard to behave in a particular way or ape someone else.
   As used in the sentence: *'Did you see her threads? Such a wannabe.'*

Waste *(way-st)* – someone who acts in an idiosyncratic way.

As used in the sentence: *'He's writing a book about birds. He's waste, but I like him.'*

Way *(w-aye)* – (1) opposite of 'no way'.

As used in the sentence: *'I've actually been allowed to stay at yours tonight.' 'Way?!'*

(2) an intensifier meaning extremely, very much, or a lot.

As used in the sentence: *'I've got some way cool news.'*

Well *(weh-ll)* – another intensifier, to exaggerate and greatly express something or someone.

As used in the sentence: *'That pasta was well good.'*

Whack/wak *(wah-k)* – crazy. An expression of surprise.

As used in the sentence: *'Are you whack? I need to cut.'*

Whatevs *(wat-evvs)* – contraction of 'whatever'; an expression of indifference.

As used in the sentence: *'She told me to go with her tonight, but I was like, whatevs.'*

▶ Usage Note: **like.**

Wodup? *(wad-upp)*– a greeting meaning, what's up? Has replaced 'Wassup!' thankfully.

As used in the sentence: *'Wodup? Lets bust a move.'*

Woop woop *(woo-p-woo-p)* – phrase used as a response to denote something as especially exciting.

As used in the sentence: *'They're moving to London – woop woop!'*

Wordage *(wer-daj)* – set of words in a written or spoken sentence.

As used in the sentence: *'Great wordage, makes you sound clever.'*

WTF *(double-you-tee-eff)* – pointless acronym for 'what the fuck?'; used to express shock or surprise. Usually said in utter disbelief.

As used in the sentence: *'YOU'RE dumping ME? WTF?'*

X – (*ex*) used as full stop at the end of texts and emails. Originated as a kiss but has become a replacement for the punctuation mark.

    As used in the sentence: *'how u x sup x call me x'*

▶ Usage Note: **sup.**

X-ray (*ex'ray*) – description of sight. Particularly relating to seeing through something/someone.

    As used in the sentence: *'Don't tell no more lies, they'll x-ray you for sure.'*

Y'all *(ya-all)* – everyone present ; contraction of 'you all'.

    As used in the sentence: *'Ready to go y'all?'*

Yard *(yah-ard)* – someone's house, property or personal space.

    As used in the sentence: *'Want to come round my hood? We can cotch in the yard?'*

Yo blad *(y-oh-bl-add)* – a manner of address; a contraction of 'yo, blood', which itself refers to 'blood brothers', kinsmen.

As used in the sentence: *'Yo, blad, coming to my yard?'*

You get me? *(yoo-get-mee)* – do you understand? Often used as an end-of-sentence filler term.

As used in the conversation: *'Let's bust a move – you get me?'*

Your mum *(yaw-muh-m)* – used as a generic retort to banter, especially to an insult. See page 114.

As used in the sentence: *'You got kaka for brains.'* *'Yeah? Your mum.'*

▶ Usage Note: **kaka.**

Yous (*yoos*) – form of address; a rare occurrence where letters are added unnecessarily as opposed to subtracted. Despite sounding plural, 'yoos' is most commonly applied to individuals.

As used in the sentence: *'Yous better watch your back or you'll find a mole growing on it.'*

▶ FYI

YOUR MUM

There is intense debate about the origins and development of the phrase 'your mum'. Shakespeare, in Act I Scene 1 of *Timon of Athens*, wrote:

> Painter: Y'are a dog.
> Apemantus: Thy mother's of my generation.
> What's she, if I be a dog?

and in Act IV, Scene 2 of *Titus Andronicus*:

> Demetrius: Villain, what hast thou done?
> Aaron: That which thou canst not undo.
> Chiron: Thou hast undone our mother.
> Aaron: Villain, I have done thy mother.

In modern culture the phrase is thought to have come from the US, such as the 1992 track by The Pharcyde, 'Ya Mama'. The Mexican film *Y Tu Mama Tambien* translates as 'And your momma too'.

Zz

Zams (*za-ams*) – exams.
　　As used in the sentence: *'I so CBA for these zams.'*

Zeds (*zeh-ds*) – sleep, coming from the zzzzzzz s illustrating sleep in cartoons.
　　As used in the sentence: *'I gotta go catch some zeds, I'm totally knackered.'*

Zip it (*zi-p it*) – shut up.
　　As used in the sentence: *'If you don't zip it, I'll wallop you.'*

ZOMG *(zed-oh-em-gee)* – a variation on the acronym OMG (Oh My God) that derived from mistakes typing 'OMG' on a keyboard: mis-reaching for the shift button for capital letters led to the letter 'z' instead, and it's usually used for a sarcastic version of OMG, to denote that something is so obvious as to not require statement.

As used in the sentence: *'So you're broke, again. ZOMG...'*

Zoned out *(zoh-nd-owt)* – daydreaming or not concentrating on the direct goings-on.

As used in the sentence: *'I totally zoned out . . . sorry . . . wagwan?'*

► Usage Note: **wagwan.**

Zonked *(zon– kd)* – tired, exhausted.

As used in the sentence: *'I totally CBA tonight – I'm zonked from getting up so early.'*

Zwah *(zw –aaah)* – a response to someone when being majorly insulted or 'owned'.

As used in the conversation: *'You've been walking around with bog roll hanging from your jeans for the last hour.' 'Zwah!'*

ZONINO

Zonino means woohoo. This is another phrase that has developed from predictive-text patterns (typing 966466 brings up zonino rather than woohoo), but – confusingly – can mean two very distinct things. Woohoo can be used as a genuine exclamation of excitement, but equally may be used as a highly sarcastic response to an authoritative figure, usually a parent or teacher, who has suggested something preposterous, such as babysitting for a sibling or turning off an iPod in a maths lesson.

As used in the conversation: *(1) 'You mean I passed my test, even though I backed into that family of garden gnomes while doing the reversing round the corner?? Zonino!'*

(2) 'You want us to go on a family camping holiday in Slough? Zonino.'

Acknowledgements

Thank you to all the friends who have helped to add, like, bare words to this book. It's been immense...

Shout out too, to Malcolm at Portico – for being way book, even when I rinsed yous for sounding old.